W9-CRX-244

WILD WATER

Water Parks

BY S.L. HAMILTON

A&D Xtreme
An imprint of Abdo Publishing / www.abdopublishing.com

Visit us at
www.abdopublishing.com

Published by Abdo Publishing Company, a division of ABDO, PO Box 398166, Minneapolis, Minnesota 55439. Copyright ©2016 by Abdo Consulting Group, Inc. International copyrights reserved in all countries. No part of this book may be reproduced in any form without written permission from the publisher. A&D Xtreme™ is a trademark and logo of Abdo Publishing Company.

Printed in the United States of America, North Mankato, Minnesota.
052015
092015

 PRINTED ON RECYCLED PAPER

Editor: John Hamilton
Graphic Design: Sue Hamilton
Cover Design: Sue Hamilton
Cover Photo: West Edmonton Mall-World Waterpark
Interior Photos: Alamy-pgs 16 & 24; Aldeia das Aguas Park Resort-pgs 14-15; AP-pgs 8, 9, 17 & 18-19; Area 47-pgs 28-29 & 30-31; Disney Parks-pg 25 (bottom); Glow Images-pgs 4-5 & 25 (top); Holiday World & Splashin' Safari-pgs 1 & 20-21; iStock-pgs 2-3 & 32; Library of Congress-pg 6 (top); Palace Entertainment/Noah's Ark-pgs 10 & 11; State Archives of Florida/Florida Memory-pg 7; Surf's Up-Nishua, NH-pgs 26 & 27; Therme Erding/Galaxy Water Park-pgs 22 & 23; West Edmonton Mall-World Waterpark-pgs 12-13.

Websites
To learn more about Wild Water action, visit booklinks.abdopublishing.com. These links are routinely monitored and updated to provide the most current information available.

Library of Congress Control Number: 2015930944

Cataloging-in-Publication Data

Hamilton, S.L.
 Water parks / S.L. Hamilton.
   p. cm. -- (Wild water)
ISBN 978-1-62403-754-2
1. Amusement parks--Juvenile literature.   I. Title.
797--dc23

2015930944

Contents

Water Parks

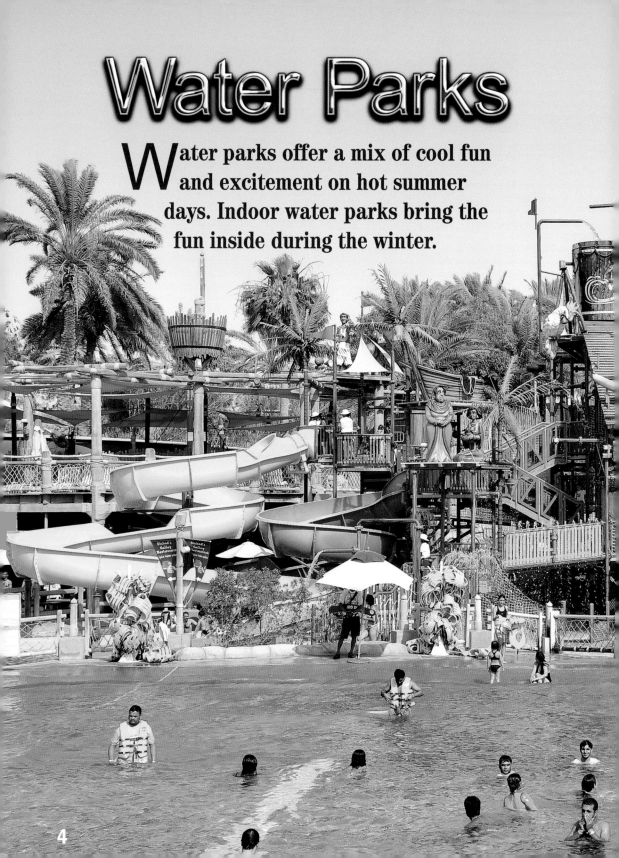

W ater parks offer a mix of cool fun and excitement on hot summer days. Indoor water parks bring the fun inside during the winter.

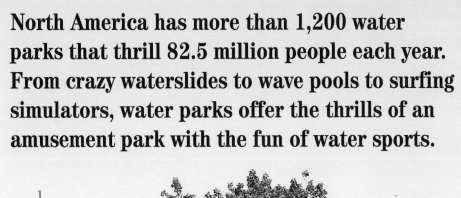

North America has more than 1,200 water parks that thrill 82.5 million people each year. From crazy waterslides to wave pools to surfing simulators, water parks offer the thrills of an amusement park with the fun of water sports.

XTREME FACT – *Walt Disney World's Typhoon Lagoon and Blizzard Beach Water Parks had more than 4 million visitors in 2013.*

History

Water slides, natural and man-made, have been a popular way to cool down and have fun for hundreds of years.

People enjoy a water toboggan slide in Put-in-Bay, Ohio, in 1904.

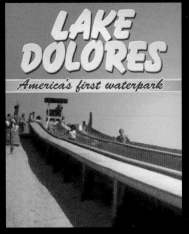

Water parks, with several different rides, are modern creations. One of the earliest was California's Lake Delores. It was created by Bob Byer for his family. He opened it to the public in 1962. It featured standing and sitting water slides, zip lines, and swings over the water.

George Millay is called the "Father of the Water Park Industry." Millay officially opened "Wet 'n Wild" in Orlando, Florida, in 1977. It featured a wave pool and a lazy river. Other developers built on Millay's success. Water and amusement park rides have combined to make fun parks around the world.

XTREME FACT – The first indoor water park opened in Wisconsin Dells, Wisconsin, at the Polynesian Resort Hotel & Suites in 1994.

Designing a Water Park Ride

Water parks appeal to many different people. Some like relaxing on a slow-moving river. Others love the thrills of water slides. Water park ride designers must know how to create a fun, safe ride.

Water slide designers are part thrill-seekers and part safety engineers. A water slide's height, how steep the drop, and the angles of curves and loops are all carefully studied. A ride must be safe for people of all sizes. Designers make water slides with high, curved sides to keep people from shooting out. A person's body may go up the side, but it must then be directed back down. Nets and enclosed slides help keep people safe.

Jeff Henry has designed more than 2,000 water park rides around the world. He stands next to "Verrückt," the world's tallest waterslide, at the Schlitterbahn Waterpark in Kansas City, Kansas.

Largest Outdoor Water Park in North America

Noah's Ark is America's largest water park. The 70-acre (28-ha) site is located in Wisconsin Dells, Wisconsin. It includes 51 waterslides, 2 wavepools, 2 endless rivers, surfing simulators, bumper boats, and more. The Scorpion's Tail and Black Anaconda are two of the wildest rides.

XTREME FACT – Wisconsin Dells, Wisconsin, is known as the Water Park Capital of the World.

The Black Anaconda is a .25-mile (.4-km) -long combination waterslide and roller coaster. Riders sit in a rubber raft that shoots them on a 30-mile-per-hour (48-kph) spiraling trip through the snake's humps and coils.

Scorpion's Tail is 10 stories high and 400 feet (122 m) long. A rider stands on a trapdoor. When it opens, the thrill seeker drops at a scream-inducing 50 feet per second (15 meters per second) to a loop that shoots them through to the end.

11

Largest Indoor Water Park in North America

World Waterpark in West Edmonton, Alberta, Canada, is the largest indoor water park in North America. It covers 5 acres (2 ha).

World Waterpark in West Edmonton, Alberta, Canada.

World Waterpark has a waterslide nicknamed "the toilet bowl." Riders on Tropical Typhoon slide down a tunnel that drops them into a funnel-shaped bowl. They circle the bowl until dropping into a 10-foot (3-m) -deep pool. The dome-covered park also has the world's largest indoor wave pool. The Blue Thunder Wave Pool holds 3.25 million gallons (12.3-million liters) of water. Waves reach heights of 5 feet (1.5 m).

XTREME FACT– The largest indoor water park in the world is Tropical Islands in Germany. It sits on more than 16 acres (6.5 ha) of land and was built on a former World War II airfield.

Tallest Free-Fall Waterslide

The tallest free-fall waterslide in the world is Kilimanjaro in Aldeia das Aguas Park Resort in Brazil, South America. Kilimanjaro stands 163 feet (50 m) tall. To get to the top, riders must climb 234 steps. In the free-fall, a person may reach speeds of 50 miles per hour (80 kph) before slowing and dropping into a pool at the bottom.

The Kilimanjaro waterslide is made of 25 tons (22.7 metric tons) of fiberglass and steel.

XTREME FACT – Kilimanjaro has an enclosed tube at the top so riders can't see the slide's full drop. Even with the view blocked, 1 in 20 people decide not to take the plunge.

Tallest Free-Fall Waterslide in North America

The tallest free-fall waterslide in North America is the Summit Plummet at Walt Disney World's Blizzard Beach Water Park in Florida. The slide looks like a 120-foot (37-m) -tall ski jump. Riders walk or take a chairlift to the top of "Mount Gushmore."

Thrill seekers begin their ride sliding through a dark tunnel. Many get a few moments of "airtime." They feel like they are floating above the water. When the tunnel ends, the rider plunges down a steep trough to a flat finish at the bottom. It takes only seconds to travel the 12 stories from top to bottom. A digital clock records a rider's speed, which ranges from 50 to 60 miles per hour (80 to 97 kph).

Tallest Raft Waterslide

Verrückt (German for "insane") is the tallest waterslide in the world. It is 168 feet 7 inches (51 m) tall. It opened at Schlitterbahn Waterpark in Kansas City, Kansas, in 2014.

Riders climb 264 steps to the top. After the 17-story climb, they are strapped into a 3-person raft. To keep anyone from flying out, the slide is encased in protective netting. The intense drop lets riders reach speeds of 60 mph (97 kph). But it's not over. At the bottom, riders are hurled up a second hill and then down a 50-foot (15-m) drop.

XTREME FACT – *Speed chuting is a German-invented sport that measures an individual's waterslide race to the bottom in milliseconds.*

Longest Water Coaster

Splashin' Safari water park in Santa Claus, Indiana, is home to the world's longest water coaster. It is called Mammoth.

XTREME FACT– Splashin' Safari is also home to Wildebeest, the second-longest water coaster. It is 1,710 feet (521 m) long.

A conveyor belt hauls up to six people on a round raft up a seven-story lift hill. In moments, riders begin the 1,763-foot (537-m) water course that takes them over seven hills and drops, including a steep 32-foot (10-m) drop at a 45-degree angle. Since the raft spins, riders may go front, back, or sideways, varying the three-minute ride every time.

Longest Inner Tube Waterslide

Galaxy Water Park in Erding, Germany, has the longest inner tube waterslide in the world. It is called the Magic Eye. The trip through the "eye" starts at a height of 72 feet (22 m). People tube through the wild, 1,168-foot (356-m) -long eye-shaped tunnel for more than a minute.

Riders twist and turn through the Magic Eye, speeding by wild light and dark areas. They end in a splashdown pool at the bottom.

Largest Outdoor Wave Pool in the U.S.

Walt Disney World's Typhoon Lagoon in Florida is the most-visited water park in the world. It contains the largest outdoor wave pool in the United States, measuring 500 feet wide by 450 feet long (152 m wide x 137 m long). It contains nearly 3 million gallons (11.4 million liters) of water.

Six-foot (2-m) waves are created every 90 seconds. A loud "sonic boom" lets people know a big surf wave is coming. Swimmers love to be carried away by each huge incoming wave.

XTREME FACT– *Up to 25 surfers can sign up to ride the waves at Typhoon Lagoon before the park opens or after it closes. The park even gives learn-to-surf lessons.*

Indoor Surfing

Surf's Up in Nashua, New Hampshire, is an indoor surf park with the world's largest standing wave machine. Surfing simulators have been making waves for riders for decades, but surfers need special boards. At Surf's Up, people use real surfboards with fins in a deep pool. Surfers shred endless 6-foot (2-m) waves, or ride barrel waves far from an ocean. They can even boogie board indoors.

A surfer in a left barrel wave.

Surfers use boards with fins at Surf's Up.

AVEMACHINES

XTREME FACT– At Surf's Up, waves can be slowed down for people just learning to surf, or sped up for big-wave surfers.

Water Catapult

Austria's Area 47 water park lets people become human cannonballs. Teens and adults take a seat aboard the Cannonball Water Catapult. When ready, the rider presses a firing button on the side of the chair. A blasting surge of water shoots the rider 33 feet (10 m) through the air to land in the lake below.

Glossary

AIRTIME
The feeling of weightlessness or coming out of one's seat when on a roller coaster or other amusement park ride.

CATAPULT
A device that hurls an object in a specific direction.

CONVEYOR BELT
A device with rollers on top of which runs a never-ending flat belt made of rubber, cloth, or metal. Conveyor belts are designed to move people or objects from one place to another.

ENGINEER
A person trained to design, build, or maintain engines, machines, or structures. Engineers design water park rides, as well as thousands of other things.

FIBERGLASS
A reinforced plastic material. Lighter than wood, fiberglass is made of glass fibers embedded in a resin. Many boats and water park rides are made with fiberglass.

SIMULATOR
A device that mimics the real thing. A surfing simulator creates waves that seem like real ocean waves.

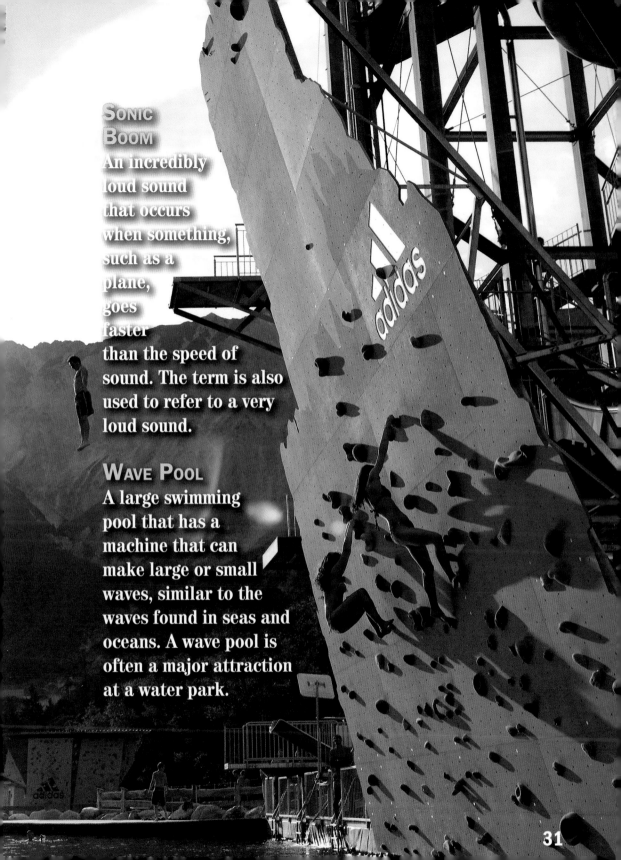

SONIC BOOM
An incredibly loud sound that occurs when something, such as a plane, goes faster than the speed of sound. The term is also used to refer to a very loud sound.

WAVE POOL
A large swimming pool that has a machine that can make large or small waves, similar to the waves found in seas and oceans. A wave pool is often a major attraction at a water park.

Index